For Andrea Lyon,
who taught my daughter when to be a lion
and when to be a lamb. Thank you.—B. M. J.

Text © 2002 by Barbara Joosse.
Illustrations © 2002 by R. Gregory Christie.

Designed by Kristine Brogno and Sara Gillingham.
Typeset in Blockhead and Officina.
The illustrations in this book were rendered in acrylic.
Manufactured in Hong Kong.

Library of Congress Cataloging-in-Publication Data
Joosse, Barbara
Stars in the darkness / by Barbara Joosse ; illustrated by R. Gregory Christie.
p. cm.
Summary: A small boy joins with his mother to find a creative way
to save his older brother from the dangers of gang violence.
ISBN 0-8118-2168-4
[1. Gangs—Fiction. 2. Brothers—Fiction. 3. Mothers and sons—Fiction.
4. Afro-Americans—Fiction.] I. Christie, R. Gregory, 1971- ill. II. Title.
PZ7.J7435St 2001
[Fic]--dc21
00-008936

Distributed in Canada by Raincoast Books
9050 Shaughnessy Street, Vancouver, British Columbia V6P 6E5

10 9 8 7 6 5 4 3 2 1

Chronicle Books LLC
85 Second Street, San Francisco, California 94105

www.chroniclekids.com

stars

IN THE
DARKNESS

BY BARBARA JOOSSE • ILLUSTRATED BY R. GREGORY CHRISTIE

Sometimes, Mama and me look down at the street and pretend it's not the city. We shut our eyes so only a crack is open, lookin' through our eyelashes, and pretend we live on the moon. The lights we see? They're stars, as many as the sky can hold. And sirens? That's wild wolves howlin' at the moon. If there's shots fired, we say it's the light of the **stars crackin' the darkness.**

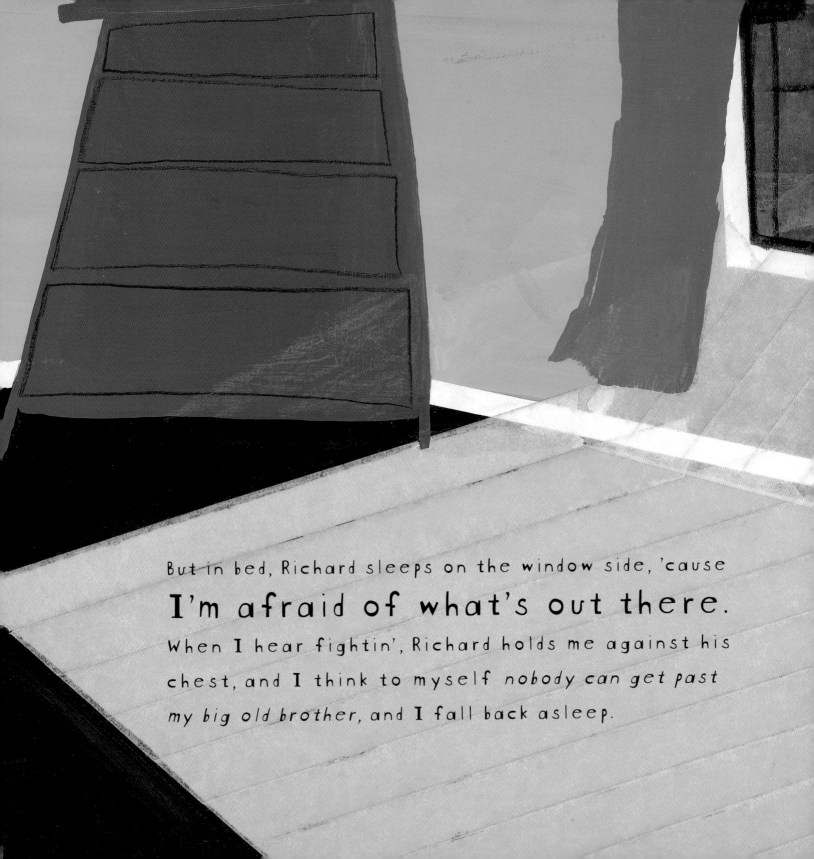

But in bed, Richard sleeps on the window side, 'cause
I'm afraid of what's out there.
When I hear fightin', Richard holds me against his
chest, and I think to myself *nobody can get past
my big old brother*, and I fall back asleep.

Lots of times, Richard and me see gang bangers on the corner. They strut around like there's tunes playin' in their heads, like they ain't afraid of nobody.

I say to Richard, "They act like they're King Stuff."

"They are," says Richard. "Nothin' can bother 'em, 'cause all the bangers are like brothers. If you mess with one banger, you mess with 'em all."

"We got each other," I say. "We sure don't need no bangers."

But tonight, Richard don't come home. There's nothin' between me and the outside. I do what I can, though. I stuff a pillow in his T-shirt and pretend it's him sleepin' next to the window.

Then I hear fightin' outside! I close my eyes and try to pretend about the stars and the wolves... but I can't, 'cause Richard's out there.

Who's fightin'? The bangers? Are they hurtin' Richard? I want to go out there and stop that fightin'. But how can I?

In the morning, **I have a bad stomach.**
Mama puts blue food coloring in the milk, to
remind me of the stars. Doesn't work, though. I
keep thinkin' about Richard.

Then Richard comes home.

Mama stands up, big as a bear.

"Boy, where you been?" she asks.

"I stayed overnight at Spanky's."

Spanky's one of the boys on the corner, but maybe Mama don't know.

"What you been doin'?" asks Mama.

"We were doin' homework, and I fell asleep on his couch."

Mama don't say nothin' more, but her face says **she don't believe him.**

A couple days later, there's a new basketball in my room. I wake Richard up. "Whose rock is that?"

Richard rubs his eyes, like he's real sleepy, but I know he's fakin' it. "What rock?"

"That new rock, sittin' on the floor. Nobody ever used that thing!"

"Ain't mine," says Richard. "Who else is livin' in this room?"

"You know!" I say. "Me."

Richard shrugs and smiles. "Must be yours then."

Where'd that rock come from, anyway? Richard don't have money.

Now, lots of times, Richard don't come
home at night. And he's walkin' that walk,
like he's King Stuff. Richard thinks I'm a
little kid, but I'm not as little as he thinks.
I know what I know.

Mama knows, too. She comes home one day
after work. She says, "Richard, you sit
down. We're havin' us a talk."

Aw, man! When Mama wants to talk, Richard's
in big trouble! I hide behind the door so
I can hear.

"What's with you hangin' with Oscar and Cisco?"

"I'm not, Mama."

"I seen you hangin' 'round with 'em ... so don't give me that! Teachers say they're gang bangers, they're wearin' colors at school." Mama grabs big old Richard and starts rockin' him back and forth, like he's a baby, way littler than me. "Don't you be hangin' out with those bangers, Richard. Don't. **Be somebody** for this world."

"I will, Mama. I will," Richard says.

Just before mornin', Richard comes to bed. I give him a hug, still half asleep, but he pulls himself away.

"Ow!" he says.

I pull the covers off and see his arm wrapped in bandages. There's blood on the bandages—*his* blood.

"I fell is all, it ain't nothin'," says Richard.

But it isn't nothin'! Like I said, I know what I know.

The next morning, I crawl up on Mama's lap. At first, we don't talk about Richard bein' hurt, bein' a banger. But we both know that's why we're rockin' each other.

Finally Mama says, "'Member how we used to pretend about livin' on the moon?" I nod.

"We can't pretend no more," she says. "We gotta be strong now."

It sure was nice, when me and Mama could pretend about the moon.

I say, "Richard's a banger, but he's still good inside. He's good to us."

"He is," says Mama, her eyes full of sad.

"So maybe the other bangers are like that, too."

"There's good and bad in everybody," Mama says.

Then Mama and me, we get us a plan.

First thing, we knock on doors and talk to the neighbors. That night, we meet on the street—the mamas and little brothers and sisters in the neighborhood. We hold hands, **so nobody's alone,** and we shine flashlights. We walk so the bangers stop fightin', stop shootin' each other. We walk so the night is not so scary.

We call 'em Peace Walks. Every night now, there's family on the streets. We take turns walkin' the night. When it's my turn, I shut my eyes so only a slit is open, and I look through my eyelashes. I see streetlights, like before, but now I see flashlights, too. Stars crackin' the darkness.

A Note from the Author

SEVERAL YEARS AGO, I met the real Richard. I liked him right away—he was strong, courageous, loyal and smart. Slowly, he began to tell me his story.

Real Richard had been a banger, a secret he kept from his family. His gang gave him a sense of power and belonging, but it gave him other things, too. Food when his family didn't have enough. Gang protection for his little brother and sister. Richard showed me his scars from gunshot wounds. What if he'd been killed? What would his family have done then?

Richard wanted out, but gang involvement was like a drug. It would take just a phone call to get back in, and Richard missed the money and power. Still, he didn't call. Now he worries that his old life will catch up with him. Will his family discover his secret? Will his employer, or the people in his new life?

Richard wanted me to tell his story. I recorded his words and played them until his street rhythms lived in my bones. Many of the details in this book are based on Richard's own experiences. Some are not, because Richard doesn't want anyone to know who he is.

I chose to write a picture book, not a novel, because I wanted to reach the little brothers and sisters. They're the ones "who know what they know." They are the stars in the darkness.

Resources on Gang Prevention

There are many resources for information on gangs and gang prevention. Below is just a partial listing. This list is for informational purposes. The philosophies and policies of these organizations and sources do not necessarily reflect those of either the publisher or the author.

Big Brothers Big Sisters of America

National Office
230 N. 13th Street
Philadelphia, PA 19107
Phone: (215) 567-7000 Fax: (215) 567-0394
Email: national@bbbsa.org

You can also contact Big Brothers Big Sisters International at www.bbbsi.org.

Provides young people ages 7 to 17 with one-on-one mentoring in areas such as school, relationships, drug use, crime and self-esteem.

The Boys and Girls Clubs of America

771 First Avenue
New York, NY 10017
Phone: (800) 854-CLUB (2582)

Offers mentoring, counseling and intervention to youth wishing to leave gangs.

Children's Aid Society

105 East 22nd Street
New York, NY 10010
Phone: (212) 949-4925

Offers counseling and mentoring programs to youth looking to leave gangs.

The Coroner's Report

http://www.gangwar.com

Information and resources on gang intervention and prevention.

Covenant House New York

460 West 41st Street
New York, NY 10036
Phone: (212) 613-0300
E-mail: chny@covenanthouse.org

Offers emergency food, clothing and shelter to young people in crisis.

Curtis High School Gang Handbook

http://www.upsd.wednet.edu/UPSD/CHS/ganghand.html

Resource guide for parents and teachers.

Gangs–A Bibliography

http://www-lib.usc.edu/~anthonya/gang.htm

Selection of books and government documents dealing with juvenile gangs, dating from 1985 to the present.

Gang Resistance Education And Training Program (G.R.E.A.T.)

http://www.atf.treas.gov/great/index.htm

Gang prevention strategy for middle-school students.

Mothers Against Gang Wars (MAGW)

http://home.inreach.com/gangbang/magw.htm

Works with schools, government and nonprofit agencies to provide children from kindergarten to high school with alternatives to violence.

National Youth Gang Center Bibliography of Gang Literature

http://www.ncjrs.org/gangbi.htm

Extensive bibliography of gang-related literature.

Omega Boys Club

P.O. Box 884463
San Francisco, CA 94188
Phone: (415) 826-8664
24-hour counseling service at (800) SOLDIER
(765-3437)

Supports young people leaving gangs and drug dealing through counseling, tutoring and college tuition funding.

A World of Prevention

http://www.tyc.state.tx.us/prevention/40001ref.html

A worldwide directory of programs, research, references and resources dedicated to the prevention of youth problems and the promotion of nurturing children.